Quickhoof and the Golden Cup

Daisy Meadows

ORCHARD

For Kirsten Fox

Special thanks to Val Wilding

ORCHARD BOOKS

First published in Great Britain in 2020 by The Watts Publishing Group

1 3 5 7 9 10 8 6 4 2

Text copyright © 2020 Working Partners Limited
Illustrations © Orchard Books 2020
Series created by Working Partners Limited

A CIP catalogue record for this book is available from the British Library.

ISBN 978 1 40836 143 6

Printed and bound in Great Britain by Clays Ltd, Elcograf S.p.A.

The paper and board used in this book are made from wood from responsible sources.

Orchard Books
An imprint of Hachette Children's Group
Part of The Watts Publishing Group Limited
Carmelite House
50 Victoria Embankment
London EC4Y 0DZ

An Hachette UK Company

www.hachette.co.uk
www.hachettechildrens.co.uk

Contents

Aisha and Emily are best friends from Spellford Village. Aisha loves sports, whilst Emily's favourite thing is science. But what both girls enjoy more than anything is visiting Enchanted Valley and helping their unicorn friends, who live there.

Quickhoof

The four Sports and Games Unicorns help to make games and competitions fun for everyone. Quickhoof uses her magic locket to help players work well as a team.

Feeling confident in your skills and abilities is so important for sporting success. Brightblaze's magic helps to make sure everyone believes in themselves!

Brightblaze

Fairtail

Games are no fun when players cheat or don't follow the rules. Fairtail's magic locket reminds everyone to play fair!

When things get difficult, Spiritmane's perseverance locket gives sportspeople the strength to face their challenges and succeed.

Spiritmane

Spellford

Enchanted Valley

Enchanted Cottage

Golden Palace

An Enchanted Valley lies a twinkle away,
Where beautiful unicorns live, laugh and play
You can visit the mermaids, or go for a ride,
So much fun to be had, but dangers can hide!

Your friends need your help ~ this is how you know:
A keyring lights up with a magical glow.
Whirled off like a dream, you won't want to leave.
Friendship forever, when you truly believe.

Chapter One
A Silvery Surprise

Emily Turner and Aisha Khan skipped joyfully ahead of their parents. It was a gloriously sunny day and they couldn't wait to watch the football match! The Spellford Seals were playing their rivals, the Greenlea Gazelles.

The Khans lived in a pretty thatched

house in Spellford called Enchanted Cottage. Aisha and Emily had met on the day Aisha's family moved in and the girls had been best friends ever since.

Emily touched the blue and gold striped scarf she wore. "Thanks for lending me a Seals scarf," she said. "I look like a real football fan."

"You soon will be," said Aisha excitedly. "The Seals' best players are Sasha Fry – she's their top striker – and Dena Walton. You should see Dena race down the wing!"

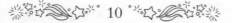

Emily grinned. "I haven't a clue what strikers and wings are, but I'm looking forward to the match," she said. "Who's your favourite player?"

"Bella Bates, the goalkeeper," said Aisha. "I'd love to be able to save goals like she does, but I'm better at passing and scoring."

"I'm no good at any of those things!" Emily sighed. "I can tell a battery clip from a crocodile clip in science, but I'll struggle with football."

"Well, I struggle in science," Aisha laughed. "We could help each other!"

Emily grinned. "Teamwork!"

"Exactly," said Aisha. "It's the team that matters, you don't need to know

individual players. The Seals are the best team ever!" She laughed again. "In my opinion, that is."

Mrs Khan handed out tickets as they joined the queue for the turnstile. Emily peered past the line and saw a grandstand on each side of the pitch. As she looked

down at her ticket to see where their seats were, a glow of light caught her eye. She drew a sharp breath, and nudged Aisha. "Your keyring," she whispered.

Aisha glanced

down at the crystal unicorn keyring that dangled from her belt. It was glowing!

Emily pulled a keyring from her pocket. "Mine's glowing, too!"

The girls knew what this meant. Queen Aurora was calling them back to Enchanted Valley!

Aisha and Emily had discovered an amazing secret in the attic of Enchanted Cottage – a crystal statuette of a unicorn. When a sunbeam shone on it, the girls were magically carried off to Enchanted Valley, a beautiful land of unicorns and other magical creatures. Aurora, the unicorn queen, had used a spell to create the crystal keyrings after their first adventure together.

The girls' eyes shone with excitement.

"Do you think this means Selena's causing trouble again?" Emily asked.

Selena was a mean unicorn who wanted to take Queen Aurora's crown and rule Enchanted Valley herself.

"If she is," Aisha said grimly, "we'll stop her. We've done it before. Come on!"

They knew that no time would pass while they were in Enchanted Valley. They wouldn't miss the match, and no one would miss them!

The girls ducked behind an ice cream kiosk and held up their keyrings. The crystal unicorns glimmered in the sunshine.

"Ready?" said Emily.

"Ready!"

They felt the
keyrings pulling
towards each other.

When the horns touched, dazzling
sparkles swirled around Aisha and Emily
– blue, pink, indigo and green. Faster and
faster the sparkles whirled, lifting the girls
right off the ground! They laughed with
excitement as Emily's long hair whipped
around her head.

As they touched down and the sparkles
started to fade, the girls knew that in a
moment they would see Queen Aurora's
glittering golden palace sitting on a
lush green hilltop, overlooking peaceful
meadows and gently bubbling streams.

"Oops, look out!" An imp wearing running shoes leaped to one side to avoid crashing into Emily.

"Coming through!" cried a little bunny, turning a series of flips.

The girls looked around them. Although they were in front of the palace, the usually peaceful grassy slopes were crowded with unicorns and magical creatures, all running, jumping, skipping or doing gymnastics. The air was filled

with excited squeals and laughter. Unicorns trotted in and out of the palace, carrying baskets of bunting, banners and balloons.

On the hillside beyond was a huge stadium of gleaming silver.

Emily's mouth dropped open. "That wasn't here last time," she said.

The stadium's delicate walls looked as if they'd been woven from strands of silvery candy floss. Flags of every colour fluttered

high above on tall silver poles.

"Cool!" Aisha gasped. "I think something sporty's happening!"

Emily grinned. "Definitely!" She pointed to the sky, where their friend Fluffy the cloud puppy was playing a game. It looked like rugby, except that his ball was a small grey raincloud. Other cloud creatures chased him, until a cloud bunny caught him and grabbed the fleecy ball. Fluffy rolled on his back and lay giggling in the air.

The cloud bunny flicked the ball with her puff of a tail. It floated down towards an elderly pixie on the ground below. The cloud bounced once, gently, on his head, then began raining on him. His eyes

widened in surprise.

Aisha giggled. "It's a cloudburst!"

They headed for the palace, passing
a team of gnomes in swimming
trunks marching towards the moat.

Chuckling pixies practising broomstick racing whizzed overhead, and a great beating of wings made the girls look up. They waved to a tumble of dragons, who were having an upside-down flying race.

Near the palace, the girls spotted their mermaid friends shrieking with laughter as they played water polo in the crystal-clear moat. The mermaids waved.

"Everyone's gone sport mad!" said
Aisha, waving back.

A unicorn came out of the palace and
trotted lightly over the silver drawbridge.
Her mane and tail were glossy gold and
her coat shimmered with the pearly
colours of a summer
dawn: pink, orange,
yellow and red.

"Aurora!" cried Emily.

The unicorn queen
wore a silver crown, and
her horn gleamed gold.
Around her neck hung
a locket with two tiny
golden suns dancing
around each other.

All the unicorns in Enchanted Valley wore magical lockets. Aurora's was the Friendship locket. While she wore it, her magic made sure that Enchanted Valley remained peaceful and friendly.

"Welcome, girls!" Queen Aurora said in her soft, lilting voice. "I'm so happy you came. We're getting ready for the Enchanted Valley Games!"

"It looks exciting!" said Emily.

"What's going to happen?" asked Aisha.

Aurora's golden mane sparkled. "Once every four years we get together to enjoy lots of different sports and fun games," she said. "This evening, at sunset, we're having a grand opening ceremony. I thought you'd like to join us."

 22

"We'd love to!" Emily said. "It looks like the sports here are a bit different from the ones we play at home."

Aurora smiled. "Some are, but there'll also be lots you know."

Hoofbeats pounded, and four unicorns cantered over the hillside towards them.

"Here are the Sports and Games Unicorns," said Aurora. "They'll be judges and referees, and they'll make sure everything goes well."

Aurora introduced them. "Quickhoof takes care of Teamwork," she said.

A unicorn with a buttercup-yellow  coat dipped her horn to say hello. Her chestnut mane and tail matched her soft brown eyes. Her locket contained a twinkling golden cup.

"Hello, Quickhoof," said the girls.

"Brightblaze is in charge of Confidence," Aurora continued, as a pearly-coloured unicorn with a scarlet mane and tail dipped her horn in greeting. Her locket had

a shining medal inside.

"Fairtail sees to Sportsmanship." A sea-green unicorn lowered her horn, and as she got up they could see her locket – a beautiful rosette.

"And Spiritmane looks after Perseverance."

A lavender unicorn with a creamy mane and tail greeted the girls. Her locket held a scroll tied with red ribbon. She was smiling but then her smile suddenly dropped and she stared over Emily's shoulder.

The girls turned to see a

small greeny-brown whirlwind moving swiftly across the meadow. The leaves twisted as it swirled along.

The whirlwind was heading straight towards them!

Chapter Two
Emily Tries

"Oh no!" cried Aisha. "Is that Selena?"

She clutched Emily's hand as the
whirlwind began to slow down. Selena
was the last person they wanted to see.
She'd be sure to ruin the Enchanted Valley
Games.

"It can't be her," Emily said, frowning.

"That whirlwind looks too small and green to be her!"

As the whirlwind came to a stop, several small creatures somersaulted to the ground. They were half as tall as the girls, with brownish-green skin which was rough and knobbly, like tree bark. Their hair seemed to be made of twigs and leaves, with little patches of bright green moss dotted here and there. Each wore a necklace of hazelnut shells, and they huddled together, holding hands.

Quickhoof and the other unicorns dipped their horns to the creatures.

"These are our friends, the wood nymphs," Aurora explained. "One of the best football teams in Enchanted Valley!"

The girls smiled and giggled in relief. "Hello!"

"*Lo*," squeaked the biggest nymph.

"*Lo*," the others echoed.

"Aisha and Emily," said Aurora, "would you like to watch the nymphs practise?"

"Yes please!" they said.

Aurora's horn glowed deep orange, sending a swish of magical stars flashing over the meadow below the hill. They cleared, leaving a flat, grassy football pitch with line markings and goals.

Tucked into one of the nets were four footballs, as white as snowberries.

The nymphs pulled strands of ivy from their pockets, and used them to tie up their twiggy hair. One nymph had trouble with a knot, so Emily stepped forward to help.

The nymph looked startled, but smiled a thank you and joined her teammates, jogging on to the pitch.

"Wood nymphs are shy," Aurora said. "They rely on each other for confidence."

Quickhoof nodded. "Confidence and trust makes them a great team."

After some warm-up exercises, the nymphs began kicking balls to each other. One nymph would call a name

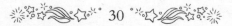

and pass the ball to that person.

Aisha saw how accurate their passes
were. The ball always landed almost at
the little wooden boot of the nymph
whose name was called ... then on to the
next.

"They're good!" Emily said. "Even I can
see that."

Suddenly, the nymphs huddled together.

"What's going on?" Emily wondered.

Aisha shrugged. "Maybe they're planning a set piece." To her surprise, the nymph who Emily had helped left the huddle and ran towards the girls.

"We wonder … would you like to join our training session?" she asked shyly.

Aisha was thrilled. "Yes, please!" She fetched a ball that had rolled off the pitch and did a few keepy-uppies. Then she dribbled it towards the nymphs.

Emily hung back. Aisha called her, but Emily gave a tiny shake of her head. "I can't," she mouthed.

Aisha ran to her.

"I've never played football," Emily said.

"I'll ruin it."

"You won't," Aisha said. "Everyone starts somewhere. It's taking part that counts! You'll soon get the hang of it."

Emily looked at the length of the pitch. "I couldn't kick a ball that far by myself," she said.

"You don't have to," said Aisha. "You're part of a team. Everyone helps everyone else. That's why we practise all that passing. Just look for someone in a space." She ran backwards, calling, "Pass to me!"

Emily took a deep breath, then kicked the ball and jumped in delight when it almost reached Aisha.

They joined the wood nymphs, who were taking turns shooting for goal.

Everyone cheered when Emily scored.

After a while, Emily noticed that the nymph she'd helped was behaving a little oddly. She was jumping around all by herself at the other end of the pitch.

"Look, Aisha," she murmured. "What on earth is she doing?"

"Sapling's the goalkeeper," Quickhoof explained. "She trains alone, because her job is different."

"I get it," said Aisha. "She doesn't need

to practise kicking goals, because she never does that in a match."

"It's a shame," said Emily. "She looks a bit left out."

Boomp! Boomp! Boomp!

Thumping and pounding shook the ground. Everyone looked puzzled. It was hard to tell where the noise came from.

Something crashed through the trees at the far side of the pitch, and out burst a huge figure.

Aisha and Emily clutched hands.

"Pitch invader!" the nymphs squealed.

A huge, hulking figure lumbered across the grass. He had a bumpy, lumpy face and flabby, outsize ears. Tufts of bristles sprouted from his head and chin, and he grunted with every step. "Gurr! Gurr! Gurr!"

"Who is that?" Aisha cried.

Quickhoof tossed her head. "An ogre!" She gave a worried glance in Aurora's direction. "What's an ogre doing here?"

Chapter Three
Popped Balls

The ogre thumped across the pitch.

The nymphs crouched behind the goal as the ogre picked up a sparkling white ball in his grimy hands. He clutched it to his chest.

"That's *my* ball!" he said in a rumbly, grumbly voice.

"It's not yours!" Aisha yelled.

"You can play with it, but you must share," Quickhoof added.

The ogre grinned, showing three large grey-green teeth. He hugged the ball tighter and giggled.

Some of the creatures ran on to the pitch and surrounded Grubb, trying to stop him from escaping with the ball.

The ogre jumped up and down crossly, but then the sky darkened.

Crash! Thunder roared, making everyone jump.

Crack! Lightning speared through dark clouds, and a unicorn flew towards the pitch. Her body gleamed silver against the grey sky, and her deep blue mane and tail flew wildly in the wind. Fluffy and his cloud friends were sent rolling and tumbling out of the way, and the racing dragons scattered, squealing.

"Selena!" Aisha gasped.

The mean unicorn flew over to Brightblaze, swooped down and shook her horn from side to side, creating a sharp breeze that whipped Brightblaze's locket from her neck. It flew to Selena and looped itself around her neck. Her hooves spat sparks as she swooped over Spiritmane and Fairtail.

"Don't, Selena!" cried Quickhoof.

One whisk of Selena's horn sent Fairtail's locket flying into the air. The same thing happened to Spiritmane's. Now Selena had three lockets draped around her neck.

She turned her purple eyes towards Quickhoof.

"Don't let her get yours as well!" Emily yelled. "Run!"

Quickhoof galloped away, but then she glanced back over her shoulder, and almost ran into the goalmouth. She

swerved, and stumbled.

Selena reared, and crackling sparks shot towards Quickhoof. In a second all four lockets were hanging beside Selena's own one, which was filled with angry black thunderclouds.

"Oh no, she got them!" Aisha cried, as Selena flew down beside the ogre. He was tossing the stolen ball into the air.

"Well, Aurora," said Selena. "That'll

stop your silly Enchanted Valley Games."

Aurora stood between her friends and the mean unicorn. "Give those lockets back."

"Ha ha!" cackled Selena. "Declare me queen and you can all have your lockets and your stupid games."

"No!" said Aurora. "If you were queen, there'd be no more games. There'd be no happiness or fun in the kingdom ever again."

"We'll never let you become queen," said Emily.

"And we'll get those lockets back," added Aisha.

Selena gave a flick of her horn. "You pesky girls?" she sneered as Quickhoof's locket flew from her own neck and dropped around the neck of the surprised ogre. "I don't think so! Grubb?"

"Yes?" he grunted.

"Leave that ball," Selena ordered, "and keep the locket well away from these fools."

Slowly, the ogre put the ball down. Then he jumped on it, bursting it with a loud *POP!* He stuck out his tongue and blew a raspberry at the girls.

"Hey!" cried Emily.

As Grubb shambled towards the forest, he jumped on the footballs, one by one.

POP! POP! POP! One of the nymphs gave a loud sob.

Selena's shriek of laughter was followed by a *crack!* as lightning zapped across the sky. She vanished.

The girls and Aurora comforted the nymphs, who were shaking with fright.

"Don't be scared," said Emily.

"Selena's gone," Aisha added.

"How can the games go on without our lockets?" asked Fairtail. All the Sports and Games Unicorns looked bewildered.

Spiritmane lifted her lavender head. "We have to try," she said. "We'll never get anywhere if we don't."

Aisha stroked her neck. "You're right, Spiritmane. We mustn't give up." She

smiled at the nymphs. "Come on," she said.

"We can't play without a ball," said Willow.

"I can fix that," said Aurora kindly. She pointed her horn at the grass. A stream of silver twinkles formed themselves into a globe. When they faded, they left behind a gleaming white ball.

The nymphs cheered up and started a kickabout. Seconds later, two of them ran for the ball at the same time and bumped into each other.

"That was mine, Leaf!" said one.

"Conifer! I got there first!" said the other.

"Didn't!"

"Did so!"

They kicked at the ball with their little wooden boots. When it rolled away, Leaf snapped, "Fetch it, Twiggy!"

"No, you kicked it."

Aisha looked at Emily and the unicorns. "Now the Teamwork locket's gone, they can't work together."

"We must sort this out," Queen Aurora said anxiously, "or soon nobody will be

able to work in a team. But I daren't
leave the palace unguarded while Selena's
around."

"We'll go after Grubb," said Emily.

Aisha shot a worried look at Emily.
"Maybe even best friends won't be able
to work together soon."

Aurora thought for a moment. "You
have my keyrings of friendship," she
said. "I'll cast a little spell to help your
friendship bond keep the effects of
Quickhoof's stolen locket at bay. First,
you must hold hands."

The queen's horn glowed deep orange,
and the air fizzed with magic. A swirl
of pastel sparkles drifted towards the
girls. They clasped hands as a ribbon of

pink, blue and lilac twisted and knotted itself around them. A magical tingle ran through their fingers.

As it faded, Aisha and Emily hugged. Their friendship felt stronger than ever.

"Now you can share the magic," Aurora told them. "If you touch someone, they will feel the bond, too. It won't last for ever, but it will help for a while."

The girls touched Quickhoof's neck, under her chestnut mane. "This is brilliant," said the unicorn. "We'll be the best team ever!"

Queen Aurora was deep in thought. "Grubb's in the forest," she said, "so it would be helpful if one of the wood nymphs went with you. They know the forest better than anyone."

"Not me!" said one of the nymphs. "That ogre is scary!"

"Me neither," declared another.

"Well, if *you* won't go, *I* won't go!" said a small nymph, crossing her arms.

Aisha frowned at Emily. It was the effect of the missing locket, for sure. "What shall we do?"

Emily thought for a moment. "I've got an idea. You can draw straws," she said. "Well, twigs, anyway." She ran to the foot of a tree and picked up a dozen thin twigs. One was shorter than the rest. She held them in her hands so only the tips showed. "Whoever picks the shortest twig comes with us," she said.

Conifer pulled out a long one, then Leaf did the same. Then it was Sapling's turn. She pulled out the short twig. The others breathed sighs of relief, but Sapling just shrugged. "I never feel like part of the team anyway," she whispered to the girls. "So – fine. Might as well go."

"Hold our hands. It will make you feel better," Aisha said.

Sapling reached up and slipped each of

her hands into the girls'. "Ooh, I do feel better!" she cried. "I feel like we can do anything together!"

Aisha and Emily shared a smile. Aurora's magic was working!

Aisha grinned. "Now, let's go and get that Teamwork locket!"

Chapter Four
Jump, Scramble, Wobble

As the friends headed for the forest, Emily kept a hand on Quickhoof's neck whilst Aisha held Sapling's hand.

"Aurora's magic will keep our friendship strong," said Emily, "but we must keep touching."

"It might get difficult at times," said

Aisha, "but we can do it."

They passed two gnomes standing on ladders, trying to hang bunting for the opening ceremony.

"Curly, your end is too high!" snapped one gnome.

"No, Hickory, your end is too low," huffed Curly, who was holding the other end of the string. He yanked the bunting upwards, sending Hickory tumbling down to the ground.

"Oof! You silly gnome!" Hickory scolded. "I should have done this by myself."

"When the locket's back, they'll work as a team again," said Emily, as they entered the forest. It was easy to see which way

Grubb had gone. He'd left a trail of fallen trees and broken branches.

"This forest is our home," Sapling said tearfully. "That nasty ogre's ruining it. He's smashing young trees and crushing ferns. What will happen to the birds and mice who live here?"

Emily hugged her. "We'll stop him," she promised. She had no idea how, but they wouldn't give up until they did.

They followed Grubb's trail, scrambling over fallen branches and slipping on squashed toadstools. All the time, they kept touching, to keep their friendship strong.

Then suddenly, *crack!* A lightning flash made them clutch each other in fright.

They looked up. Selena hovered overhead, grinning down at them.

Sapling pressed close to Emily, who shouted, "What now, Selena?"

The evil unicorn clapped her front hooves together, sending a shower of burning sparks to the ground. Emily and Quickhoof stamped on them.

"That's dangerous!" Aisha yelled. "You could set the forest on fire!"

"Ha! That would stop you following Grubb," laughed Selena. "But I've something better than that. If you all think you're so great at sports, try tackling my obstacle course!" Her laughter echoed through the treetops as she flew away.

"What obstacle course?" Sapling asked nervously.

But as they followed the narrow path around a bend, the answer was in front of them: a twisted tangle of spiky tree branches. Beneath them was a net of thick knotted vines! Fat yellow berries grew among the vines, and each one had a sharp, curved thorn on top.

"Clawberries!" said Sapling. "They

grow on Selena's mountain. They'll rip your clothes if they get half a chance."

"It looks like we have to crawl under that net," said Emily. "Be careful, everyone."

They gripped on to one another tightly and scrambled under the net.

"Ouch!" said Quickhoof as a clawberry snagged her mane.

"Eek, this is hard," Sapling moaned as a clawberry scratched her arm.

"Let's take turns holding the net up for each other with our spare hands," Emily suggested.

"Good idea," said Aisha.

"I'll use my horn," said Quickhoof.

They took turns, first holding the net

up, then scrambling through. They had
to keep touching each other and, at the
same time, keep away from the berries'
sharp claws.

At last they made it.

A little way ahead lay a half-fallen tree,
with thick thorny weeds growing around
it. Aisha went to push past it, through the
weeds.

"No!" cried Sapling, pulling her back.
"Those weeds are itchy-scratchies. If you
touch them the itching will drive you
wild."

"This must be the next obstacle, then,"
Emily said. "We'll have to walk along
the trunk without touching the itchy-
scratchies, then jump off." She peered

through the trees. It looked like the trunk sloped upwards. "It could be quite a drop at the far end." She looked at Quickhoof. "Maybe you … ?"

The unicorn shook her head. "I can't fly you over. Look, the tree branches are quite low, and the itchy-scratchies have grown up into them."

"Why don't we go in pairs?" Aisha suggested. "Sapling, you go with Emily and then Quickhoof and I will follow."

Emily held Sapling's hand and clambered on to the tree trunk. "Whoooa!" she cried. "It's wobbling." She slipped, dropping Sapling's hand.

Aisha reached up and grasped Sapling's hand. "Oh dear, it looks like we need to

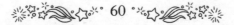

use our arms to balance. We'll have to go
one at a time."

"What about our friendship bond?"
asked Quickhoof.

"Aurora's spell is protecting Emily and
me," said Aisha, "so we'll be all right.
Quickhoof and Sapling, you'll just have
to be fast. I'll go first and test it out."

Aisha stepped up on to the trunk,
holding her arms out wide. She moved

carefully, as if she was on a balance beam in gymnastics class, putting one foot directly in front of the other. She reached the end and leaped down, landing with a thud.

"Bend your knees when you land," she called back to the others. "The ground's rock-hard."

Quickhoof went next. As soon as Emily took her hand off the unicorn's neck, she started grumbling. "I'd get along much better on my own," she said as her hooves clip-clopped along the trunk. "The rest of you are holding me back."

As soon as the unicorn jumped down, Aisha stroked her neck.

"Oh no! Sorry I was rude," said

Quickhoof. "It's because the magic left
me when I let go …"

"We know," Aisha said gently.

Emily lifted Sapling on to the tree
trunk, and as soon as she let go Sapling
began to moan. "Don't see why I should
do this. Why couldn't someone else go?
Why me?"

She ran lightly along the trunk, but
stopped at the end. "I'm not jumping.

That drop is way too high!"

"I'll catch you," Aisha promised.

Sapling scowled. "You'd drop me. Anyway, I don't need help from you!"

Emily climbed up and ran along the trunk, up behind Sapling. She tried to catch Sapling's hand, but the nymph snatched it away and leaped off the tree, away from Aisha. She stumbled as she landed.

"Ow! My ankle!" she cried.

Aisha lifted her up. As soon as they touched, Sapling burst into tears. "I'm sorry I was horrible. I didn't mean it!"

"We know," said Emily. "It's the magic's fault."

Sapling took a step and yelped. "It

hurts! I can't walk!"

"Poor Sapling," said Aisha. She put an arm around the nymph to support her.

Emily did the same, then she looked at Aisha over Sapling's head and said quietly, "Now what do we do?"

Chapter Five
A Wild Ride

Quickhoof nuzzled Sapling's forehead.
"You can ride on my back," she said.

Emily and Aisha boosted Sapling up.
Emily kept her hand on Quickhoof's neck
whilst Aisha held on to Sapling's good
ankle.

"Great!" said Emily. "We'll soon catch

Grubb and get the locket back. It should be easier going now."

But they had only walked a short way when Quickhoof stopped suddenly. Her ears twitched. "Listen."

A rushing sound came from just over a rise ahead.

"What's that?" Aisha said with a worried frown.

They scrambled over the rise and saw a fast-flowing river.

"Wow! That's three times as wide as the palace moat," said Quickhoof.

There were rapids, too, where the water surged and pounded over hidden rocks.

Emily spotted a movement way downriver. It was the lumbering, hulking

figure of the ogre on a little raft. "After him!" she cried.

"How?" asked Quickhoof.

Aisha gave a delighted shout and pointed to the water's edge. A raft with four paddles bobbed on the river. A rope of vines tied it to a tree.

"Come on!" she cried. "We can use that raft to catch up with Grubb. But be sure to keep touching each other, so we work

as a team."

They climbed aboard the raft. Emily sat with Sapling behind her, and Quickhoof sat behind Aisha.

Emily leaned over and pulled the vine free. Everyone tumbled backwards as the raft shot out into the middle of the river.

"Keep the raft balanced," Emily cried, "otherwise we'll tip over."

Aisha and Emily paddled, while Sapling and Quickhoof held on to them. But the raft seemed to have a mind of its own. The girls weren't strong enough to control it.

"We need more paddle power!" cried Aisha as the raft bounced off a rock and wobbled dangerously. "It'll mean letting go of each other, but let's risk it."

Sapling picked up an oar and Quickhoof took the last one in her mouth.

"Paddle hard!" cried Aisha, as they hurtled downriver. "Grubb's heading back towards the bank."

"Padda iss ay!" Quickhoof shouted to Sapling.

"Can't understand you with your mouth full," yelled Sapling. "Paddle this way!"

The raft crashed sideways into a huge rock, and Quickhoof's paddle was knocked out of her mouth. She tried paddling with her hooves but they were too dainty. Sapling, meanwhile, was

paddling backwards, making the raft go
around in circles.

"That's the wrong way, Sapling!" Emily
shouted.

"No, *you're* all going the wrong way,"
Sapling yelled.

"It's out of control!" cried Aisha.

"Hold tight, everyone!" Emily yelled, as
the raft tipped dangerously. They gripped
the sides, but Quickhoof couldn't hold

on and rolled towards Sapling. The raft
overbalanced and, with a huge *SPLASH*,
they were in the water.

Aisha and Emily plunged deep into
the river. Luckily both were good
swimmers and when they bobbed
up, they saw Sapling and Quickhoof
already scrambling out on to the bank,
soaking wet. The raft had whirled away
downriver, far out of reach.

Quickhoof groaned.

"Are you hurt?" Emily called as she crawled up the bank and turned to help Aisha.

"No," said the unicorn. "As I swam ashore, I saw Grubb. On the other bank of the river."

The girls could see that she was right. The ogre's trail of destruction continued on the far side.

Behind them Sapling grumbled, "It's Quickhoof's fault!"

The unicorn stamped. "I'm fed up with this!" she said. "I don't need you lot. I'll fly over the river on my own, and I'll get the locket back myself!"

"No!" cried Emily, leaping forward.

"You'll need our help!"

"Touch her!" Aisha yelled.

But Quickhoof took off and flew swiftly across the river.

Emily hugged Sapling as Aisha stared after the unicorn.

"This is bad," Aisha said. "Quickhoof won't manage to deal with Selena and Grubb on her own."

Quickhoof landed on the bank and disappeared into the trees ... along with any hope of getting back the locket.

Chapter Six
Not Another Challenge!

Emily, Aisha and Sapling sat on the
riverbank, holding hands.

"How can we cross the river?" Aisha
wondered gloomily. "I wish we could fly."

"Hmm ..." Emily said. She sat up.
"Maybe we can! Sapling, how do you
do that whirlwind thing? You know, like

when you arrived at football practice?"

Sapling shrugged. "We hold on tightly to each other, then we run round and round as fast as we can and then we say the magic words to make a whirlwind and take off. We shout out where we want to go and we usually tumble over when we land."

Aisha felt a twinge of hope. "Could your whirlwind carry us?"

"Maybe," Sapling said, "but I can't run with my hurt ankle."

Emily's eyes sparkled with excitement. "If you put your arms across our shoulders," she said, "we'll support you. We do the running, you do the magic! How about it?"

Sapling grinned. "Let's give it a go!"

The girls held her up, with Sapling's arms gripping their shoulders and her little legs dangling between them. Then Aisha took a deep breath. "When I say go, Emily, we must run in a circle as fast as we can. One ... two ... three ... GO!"

They ran around and around.

"Keep going!" cried Sapling.

Everything became a blur.

"Faster!" the nymph cried. *Swooooosh!*

The girls felt their feet leave

the ground. "Wooo!" Emily yelled in excitement. It was weird running in mid-air.

They heard Sapling shout, "Whirly wind and windy whirl, over the river – twirl, twirl, twirl!" Then she said, "Nearly there, girls, slower … slower … careful …"

They somersaulted to the ground in a dizzy, giggling heap.

"That was amazing!" said Aisha. She tried to stand. "Ooh, I'm woozy!"

Emily blew her hair out of her eyes. "My head's spinning!"

Once the dizziness had cleared, the friends hurried off through the forest. The girls carried Sapling between them, her arms around their shoulders.

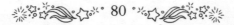 80

They skirted a
thicket of purple
tangleweed and
emerged into
a clearing. On
the far side was
Quickhoof. She
was pawing
the ground and
tossing her head crossly. The girls could
see why. Selena and Grubb were standing
on a rock shaped like a platform, looking
down on Quickhoof and teasing her.

"Want your locket, do you?" Selena
sneered.

"It's *my* locket now," the ogre taunted.

"It's not yours!" Emily shouted.

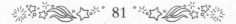

Quickhoof turned. She glared at the friends and snorted grumpily. "Go away! I can handle this on my own!"

"You can't!" Aisha yelled.

"Let us help you!" Emily added.

Lifting Sapling between them, the girls ran to Quickhoof and put their hands on her neck.

Quickhoof's head drooped right away. "I'm sorry," she said, with a sob in her voice. "I didn't mean to be horrible. It's because I've lost my locket."

Grubb laughed. "I told you, it's *my* locket!"

Selena shoved him off the rock. "You lot got through my obstacle course," she said with a sly look in her purple eyes, "but I have another game for you."

The girls sighed. "Why would we play against you?" Aisha said, hands on hips.

"Because if you win, you get the locket back," Selena said. "But if my team wins, you get Aurora to step down and make me queen. Deal?"

Emily looked at Aisha. "We've no choice."

"Deal," Aisha told Selena. "What game?"

In reply, Selena reared up and electric sparks ran over her silver body. Then – *fffzzzaaaappp!* – a bolt of lightning shot across the clearing, and – *pow!* – a football pitch appeared. But it was nothing like the rich green one Aurora

had conjured up. There was no grass, just stinky, swampy black mud.

Selena jumped off the rock and touched her horn to the hairy spot between Grubb's eyes. Four bright flashes shot out from it and hit the ground. *Zzzap!* Four

more ogres appeared, identical to Grubb.

They giggled together, flapping their ears. Only the Teamwork locket around Grubb's neck showed which one he was.

"Five-a-side football," said Selena.

"Fine," said Aisha. At least it was a game she knew.

"There's only three of us!" Emily whispered urgently.

"Four," said Sapling. "I'll be in goal. At least I won't have to run on my ankle."

"We'll still beat the Grubbs," Aisha insisted. "Right, team?"

Sapling and Quickhoof both said a shaky, "Right."

"But if we let go of each other," Emily said, "we won't work as a team."

Aisha looked into Emily's eyes. "We. Can. Do. This."

"But …" Emily wasn't so sure.

Sapling pulled at Aisha's sleeve. "There's no referee," she said. "Those Grubbs will cheat."

"Oh, you've got a referee," Selena cackled. "Me!" She tossed her head and a whistle appeared, hovering in front of her mouth.

Emily groaned. "This will be *impossible*!"

Chapter Seven
Friends v Grubbs

The game was a struggle from the first whistle blast, when an ogre shoved Emily over and banged the ball into the net. 1–0.

Emily picked herself up from the mud and saw Aisha haring down the pitch, dodging the lumbering ogres.

"Shoot!" yelled Sapling, who was leaning on her goal post, resting her ankle.

Wham! Aisha slammed the ball into the ogres' goal. 1–1!

Selena blew her whistle. "Free kick to Team Grubb!"

"Why?" Aisha demanded.

Selena raised an eyebrow and grinned. "Because I say so."

Grubb took the kick and scored. 2–1

to the ogres. They kicked off again, but
Aisha slipped between a Grubb's legs,
whipped the ball away, raced down the
wing and scored! As the ball hit the net,
Selena blew the whistle.

Phweee!

"Goal disallowed!" she screeched. "You
didn't bow to me before you kicked."

Quickhoof flew over. "Selena, you're
making up rules as you go along!"

Selena blew a whistle blast. "So?"

"You can't do that," Emily yelled.

"Yellow card for answering back," Selena snapped.

The ogres had got the ball and were thundering down towards the friends' goal. Aisha ran out, tackled and got possession of the ball. She passed to Emily, who passed to Quickhoof. The unicorn dribbled past Grubb, heading for the goal.

Phweee!

"Foul!" bellowed Selena. "Free kick to the Grubbs!"

Sapling hopped up and down crossly. "Unfair!" she shouted.

Selena trotted over. "Yellow card for being rude to the ref," she said, holding it right up against Sapling's nose.

The game got harder still when Selena used magic to make the friends' goal bigger and the Grubbs' goal smaller. Sapling was too little to save many goals, and the Grubb goalie practically filled his net.

Luckily, whenever Aisha did manage to get the ball, she took a shot at goal.

The score was 9–8 to the Grubbs, when Selena shouted, "I'm fed up with this." She took a deep breath to blow her whistle, but just before she did, Aisha kicked the ball away from a Grubb and booted it between the goalie's legs into the net.

Goal!

"You must allow that one, Selena," said Emily. "It's a draw!"

Selena scowled. "Fine! Each team gets one penalty kick. Whoever scores, wins."

"Great," said Aisha. "I'm good at penalties."

"Grubbs first," Selena said spitefully. "It'll save you bothering."

Sapling stood in goal, looking very tiny.

The real Grubb shambled halfway up the pitch, turned and began his run-up, grunting at each step. "Get ready!" He swung his foot at the ball and booted it with all his might straight for the top corner of the goal.

Sapling was ready. She leaped, stretched out her arms and grabbed the ball safely with both hands. She landed, clutched her ankle and gave a yelp.

 92

"Poor Sapling," said Aisha. "Are you going to be OK?"

Sapling just pouted and hobbled to the sidelines.

"We should help her," said Emily, "but we have to get the locket first. This is our final chance. Aisha, you're up."

Aisha ran to the penalty spot. As she did, the Grubb nearest her took a dive.

"Ow!" he roared. "She stamped on my little toe. Ow!"

Selena shoved a red card in Aisha's face, pointed to the side of the pitch and

snapped, "Off!"

"Off! Off! Off!" chanted the Grubbs.

It meant Aisha couldn't take the shot.

"Cheats!" Emily said.

Aisha looked at Emily, eyes wide. "Sapling can't kick with her bad ankle," she said. "Quickhoof won't find it easy with hooves. It must be you!"

Emily gulped.

"You can do it!" Aisha insisted. "You think you can't, but you can."

"Let's hope so," muttered Sapling.

Aisha ignored her and put the ball on the spot. "All you have to do, Emily," she said, "is think positively. Believe in yourself and boot it!"

Emily took a deep breath and eyed

the ball. She ran – and kicked. It flew through the air and curved down, down towards the net. The ogre dived to the right, and the ball slammed deep into the left corner of the net.

"Goooaaalll!" Aisha screamed. "We won! Well done, Emily!"

The girls went straight up to the real Grubb and Emily held out her hand. "The locket, please."

The ogre's face fell. "I never wanted it anyway," he snapped, and took it off.

Selena screeched angrily. "Don't give it to her," she said. "I've changed my mind."

Emily gasped. "You can't do that!"

"Oh yes I can," Selena said. "And I'll be able to do whatever I like when I'm queen."

"We'll see about that!" Aisha fumed. She booted the ball straight at Grubb's hand. The locket flew out of his hand and over their heads.

Everyone turned to see a little green and brown figure leap up and snatch the locket out of the air.

The girls clapped and cheered. "Well saved, Sapling!"

Chapter Eight
Friendship For Ever!

Quickhoof flicked her horn, sending showers of sparkles towards the golden cup locket in Sapling's hand. It rose up, drifted towards Quickhoof and draped itself around her neck.

Selena shrieked in fury. Her deep blue mane sent out flashes of green light.

Emily and Aisha held out their arms
to Sapling and Quickhoof. The unicorn
bent to rub her velvety cheek against the
girls' faces, and Sapling hobbled over. The
magic was back.

"Team hug!" Emily yelled.

"Sorry I was awkward," said
Quickhoof.

"And sorry I was moody," said Sapling.

"No, I'm sorry," said Aisha.

Emily laughed. "We're all sorry! And

we're all friends again."

They jumped up and down in delight, but stopped when Sapling winced. "Silly ankle," she said.

Quickhoof offered her a ride until they could find someone to look at her poor foot.

"Thanks. That's kind," said Sapling.

"It's what friends are for," said Quickhoof, "to help and support each other."

The girls lifted Sapling up, and she buried her hands in Quickhoof's chestnut mane.

Selena galloped over and slid to a stop. "Fine! You've got your stupid Teamwork locket, but just remember, I've still got the

other three. Ha! You'll never get those."

She stamped her front hooves, then leaped into the air amid crashing thunder and flashing, crackling lightning.

"Our friendship's too strong for you!" Emily yelled.

Quickhoof said to the girls, "Jump up behind Sapling."

The girls shivered with excitement. They never got used to the thrill of flying! As Quickhoof soared into the sky, they held each other tightly.

"Friendship for ever!" cried Aisha.

The others echoed her, their words whipping away on the wind. "… for ever!"

As Quickhoof swooped down, they saw

that the silver stadium and the grounds around the palace were as busy as before.

"Everyone's working together!" Emily shouted happily.

As they landed, Aurora came to meet them. "Congratulations!" she cried. "We knew Quickhoof had her locket back because everyone suddenly started being friendly and working as a team again. Thank you!"

Aisha and Emily jumped off Quickhoof's back and helped the little nymph down.

"We couldn't have done it without Sapling," said Aisha. "She saved the locket!"

Emily patted the nymph on her twiggy

head. "She saved the day!"

"And the goal!" said Quickhoof.

A crowd gathered to congratulate the friends, and Sapling's teammates hugged their goalie. She looked surprised, but

pleased, too!

Emily whispered to Aisha, "I don't think she's ever had attention like this before."

The nymphs' team captain heard and said, "Everyone, please listen!" She turned to Sapling. "It's easy for us to forget how important our goalie is. But we always appreciate you, Sapling. We'll make sure you take part in all our practices. You don't *need* to practise shooting, but it's good for the team to be together. You'll help us bond. That's the important thing."

Everyone clapped, and Aisha shouted, "Three cheers for Sapling, the nymph of the match! She's saved the Enchanted Valley Games. Hip hip!"

"Hooray!"

Cheers echoed around Enchanted Valley as Aurora stepped forward. Her golden horn sent a stream of deep red sparkles straight into Aisha's hand.

The sparkles cleared to reveal a scarlet pouch, tied with a fine golden thread.

"There's something in there that will help Sapling's hurt ankle," Aurora explained.

Aisha opened the pouch, and Emily took out a strip of glistening, gold-tipped lichen. She wrapped it around Sapling's ankle.

The little nymph wiggled her foot. She stood on it. She jumped on it. "It's better!" she cried. "Thank you, Queen

Aurora. And thank you, Aisha, Emily and Quickhoof. You've helped me make so many friends." She looked around at the crowd, who cheered again.

Aurora said to the girls, "The sun's nearly set."

Emily nodded. "It's time for us to go," she said. "We're sorry to miss the opening ceremony."

Aurora's eyes twinkled. "You won't," she said. "The Enchanted Valley Games can't go ahead until we have all the stolen lockets back. Will you come again and help us find them?"

The girls hugged her. "Of course we will," they said.

"I know I can count on you," said

Aurora. "I'll call you soon. Goodbye."
Her horn glowed deep orange, spilling
sunshine sparkles that swept around the
girls, bathing them in golden light. As
they felt their feet leave the ground, they
shouted, "Bye!!"

Moments later, the sparkles faded. The
girls felt firm ground beneath their feet
again, and heard football fans chanting
"Spellford Seals for ever!" Emily and
Aisha ran out from behind the ice cream
kiosk and hurried to take their seats with
their parents.

Ten minutes after the match began, the
Greenlea Gazelles' striker shot for goal.
The ball headed straight for the crossbar,
but Bella Bates, the Seals' goalkeeper,

leaped high in the air and punched it backwards over the goal net.

Aisha and Emily cheered.

"Spectacular!" said Mrs Khan, as the whole team hugged Bella.

Mr Turner said it was the finest save he'd ever seen. "She'll be player of the match, I'll bet," he said.

Emily and Aisha both spoke at once. "The team's the most important thing!"

Mrs Khan laughed. "You two seem to be quite a team," she said.

The girls shared a smile. They were part of a much bigger team – the friends of Enchanted Valley.

The End

Join Emily and Aisha
for more fun in ...

Brightblaze Makes a Splash

Read on for a sneak peek!

Aisha Khan stood outside her classroom door with her best friend Emily Turner, wishing she was anywhere else in the world.

"I don't know if I can do this," she whispered.

Emily squeezed her hand comfortingly and said, "It's only a book report."

Aisha fiddled with the bookmark in her copy of *Black Beauty*.

The two friends both loved the book. They must have read it a hundred times. But while Emily felt confident in the classroom, Aisha was more at home outside on the sports fields. This book report was giving her butterflies in her tummy.

She groaned and leaned against the wall. "I wish Black Beauty would come so I could ride away!"

Read
Brightblaze Makes a Splash
to find out what's in store
for Aisha and Emily!

Also available

Book Nine:

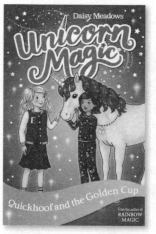

Daisy Meadows

Unicorn Magic

Quickhoof and the Golden Cup

From the author of RAINBOW MAGIC

Book Ten:

Daisy Meadows

Unicorn Magic

Brightblaze Makes A Splash

From the author of RAINBOW MAGIC

Book Eleven:

Daisy Meadows

Unicorn Magic

Fairtail & the Perfect Puzzle

From the author of RAINBOW MAGIC

Book Twelve:

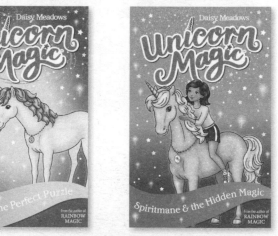

Daisy Meadows

Unicorn Magic

Spiritmane & the Hidden Magic

From the author of RAINBOW MAGIC

Unicorn Magic

Look out for the next book!

Daisy Meadows

Unicorn Magic™

Brightblaze Makes a Splash

From the author of
RAINBOW MAGIC

Visit
orchardseriesbooks.co.uk
for

✴ fun activities ✴

✴ exclusive content ✴

✴ book extracts ✴

There's something for everyone!